I Will Always Love You

Written by Carline Dumerlin-Folkes

Illustrated by Lea Embeli

ISBN: 1979725764
ISBN-13: 978-1979725767

Dedication

To my two bears, Andrew and Greg

To Lisa, thank you for encouraging me

During the summer or the cool,
orange-colored fall,

I will always love you and I will be there whenever you call.

On rainy days or on days when the sun shines bright,

I will always love you and I will be there to tell you goodnight.

When you are happy or if you are ever sad,

I will always love you and will lend a helping hand.

When you sing, dance or clap,
even if it is a bit off-key,

I will always love you, you mean the world to me.

When you draw or color, a house,
a flower or a bee,

*I will always love you, your art is
a masterpiece to me.*

When you are scared or if you feel alone,

I will always love you, we can talk and share an ice cream cone.

When you learn to ride a bike, start pre-school or fly a kite,

I will always love you, your future is very bright.

If you ever join a club or try-out for a team,

I will always love you, you are always number one to me.

Over the moon and beyond the stars,

I will always love you, whether you are near or far.

I Will Always Love You **Sight Words**

a	fall	me
all	for	sing
are	fly	the
always	I	tell
be	if	warm
call	is	you

Sight words are words that are usually memorized to help a child learn to read and write.

About the Author

Carline Dumerlin-Folkes is an avid reader whose love for books began at an early age. With many years of experience in the field of education, Carline is dedicated to helping people develop into their best selves. She is also the author of the book, Kiss the Sky: *Reflections on Becoming Your Best Self.*

Made in the USA
Lexington, KY
09 March 2018